Dan's Lost Hat

HAMERAY
PUBLISHING GROUP

Dan has lost
his flying hat.
He looks under the bed.
He looks under the mat.

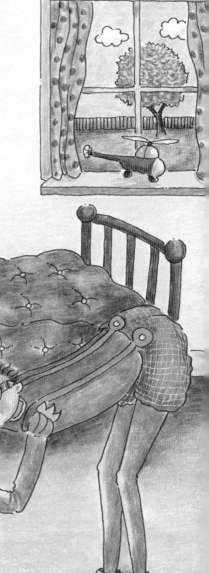

He looks on the shelf.
He looks on the chair.
He looks in the fridge.
He looks everywhere.

Dan is feeling sad.

His day has turned out bad.

He can't find his flying hat,
so he can't fly, and that is that!

Soon the news gets around.

The flying hat cannot be found.

A man says, "Dan, I'm sad for you.
I am sad for myself, too.
You have lost your flying hat,
and I have lost my tabby cat."

At that moment, the people stare
at something whizzing through the air.

It's a large and fluffy tabby cat
and it is wearing Dan's flying hat!

"Come down!" cries the man.

"Come down!" cries Dan.
"Please come down, you tabby cat.
You have on my flying hat!"

Cries go up all over town.
"Come down, Cat. Come down!
Come down!"

Dan is quick
to think of a trick.

He puts some fish
in a cat food dish.

ZOOM!

Down comes the cat
in two seconds flat!

The man gets back his tabby cat,
Dan gets back his flying hat,
and the cat gets tasty fish
heaped up in a cat food dish.